Revenge of the Dolls

I went
outside

Revenge of the Dolls

by
CAROL BEACH YORK

Weekly Reader Books
Middletown, Connecticut

Published in the United States by Elsevier/Nelson Books, a division of Elsevier/Dutton Publishing Company, Inc., New York. Published simultaneously in Don Mills, Ontario, by Thomas Nelson and Sons (Canada) Limited.

Xerox Education Publications paperback book-club edition published by arrangement with Elsevier/Nelson Books.

  2 3 4 5 / 84 83 82 81 80

XEROX ® is a trademark of Xerox Corporation.

For my dear friend
Marge Barkan

Revenge of the Dolls

Chapter 1

I REMEMBER that December afternoon as clearly as if I were there again now in the living room trimming the tree with Trissy. Light glowed and glimmered in the ornaments. Outside snow was falling. Mama sat on the couch opening Christmas cards that had just come in the mail.

I can still hear the soft sliding sound of cards coming from envelopes.

"Cousin Grace." Mama leaned forward and handed a card to Daddy.

"There's a note on the back," Mama added. "Aunt Sarah hasn't been feeling well. The cold weather, I suppose."

Daddy lifted an eyebrow. He thought there was a lot more wrong with Mama's Aunt Sarah than cold weather could account for. But he didn't argue. He was feeling lazy and content in the warm Christmas room. Aunt Sarah was too far away to worry about.

"Grace wonders if I could possibly get out for a visit before summer."

I hung a silver trumpet on a high branch. Only Daddy could reach the top, to put on the star.

"Actually, it might not be bad to go in the spring this year, when the girls have their spring vacation," Mama said thoughtfully. "It's always so hot at Aunt Sarah's in the summer."

Whether we went in spring or summer, I didn't look forward to the visit. An air of gloom always hung over Aunt Sarah's house—over the gardens and porches, in the shadowy corners of the high-ceilinged rooms. A sense of something I didn't understand pervaded the house where Aunt Sarah lived, with Cousin Grace to take care of her, and a hired girl from town to cook and clean.

Mama thought Aunt Sarah was harmless. A harmless old lady. "A little eccentric," was the most Mama would concede.

10

Daddy thought Aunt Sarah was quite mad, crazy as a loon. Harmless, maybe . . .

Oh, Daddy, if you only knew. Am I the only one who really knows?

In a room far away, Cousin Grace had sat at her desk. I could imagine her, neat and drab and growing old. Carefully, in a thin, spare script, she had signed our Christmas card, addressed the envelope, reached for a stamp in the shallow desk drawer with the brass lion-head knob. Probably she was alone in the living room; Aunt Sarah so rarely came downstairs.

And then on the back of the card Cousin Grace had added a note. She wondered if Mama could come sooner than summer.

Daddy laid Cousin Grace's card in the basket with the other cards. I looked at it later. Silver and gold. Angels and stars. It had come from a snowbound house in the midst of a wintry countryside, come from a place I did not know. I only knew Aunt Sarah's house in summertime . . . and oh, I knew the summers well. Mosquitoes by the Queen Anne's lace, the creak of porch chairs, the slam of the back-door screen, shades drawn to keep the rooms cool, afternoon lemonade, the musty smell of the grape arbor with its sprawling vines and dark leaves, sunlight shimmering on the black asphalt road to town, birds scolding squirrels in the tree branches.

But as I held the card, I thought I could imagine this winter place, this place I had never seen. I could imagine the garden covered with snow, the ground frozen hard, dead stalks where flowers had been, fires burning in the fireplaces, and bitter wind sweeping against the windows.

Somehow, with the arrival of the card, the gloomy presence of Aunt Sarah's house had also come. I could feel it close silently about me in the room that had been so perfect, so bright and Christmasy. Was I the only one who felt the change?

Trissy threw icicles at the tree, and Mama said, "Don't throw, darling." Only Mama had the patience to put each silvery strand on separately, hanging it straight, perfectly positioning it. *I love you, Mama.* . . . We need people who are willing to do things carefully, patiently, perfectly. Everything would be so disorderly without people like Mama.

But, oh, Mama—we should have gone in the

summer, as we always did. Things might have been different then.

Mama had taken up her copy of *A Christmas Carol*, and Trissy was snuggling beside her on the couch. Could Trissy understand the Ghost of Christmas Past?

"Marley was dead, to begin with." Mama's voice was soft, lilting. The tree lights glowed. Snow fell at the windows.

Marley was dead, to begin with.

Read that again, Mama: Aunt Sarah was mad, to begin with.

Chapter 2

I NEVER DID see Aunt Sarah's house in the wintertime.

I never saw the garden deep with snow, the ice formed between the flagstones of the path leading to the grape arbor. I never saw the woods silent and white. I never saw the road to town blown over with drifting snow, that winter place from which the Christmas card had come.

But I did at last see fires in the big old-fashioned fireplaces with brick hearths and clocks chiming on the mantelpieces.

We went for a week in early spring—Mama, Trissy, and I, and the weather was damp and chill. There was always a fire in the living room, and I liked to sit beside it and watch the flames. The blazing fire made the whole room beautiful. Light glowed on the polished table-tops, the brass jardinieres, the oil paintings in their heavy frames.

And there was always a fire in Aunt Sarah's room upstairs. But the fire was less welcoming there. It cast mysterious shadows on the carpet, on the dark furniture, on the faces of the dolls—and made their glass eyes gleam like the eyes of wolves on the fringes of a campfire.

Cousin Grace came to meet our train. I saw her first, a thin, melancholy woman in a beaver coat. The rails were silvery with rain as the train ground to a stop, and through the rain-streaked windows I could see Cousin Grace appear in the dusk like an apparition with her dark eyes and pale cheeks. Her face floated there in the misty light, and I drew back from the window silently, though I had been about to cry out, "There she is, Mama. I see Cousin Grace."

Later Trissy and I sat in the back of the car, lost on the wide, velvety, dove-gray seat. No one had ever used the ashtrays set into the doors. No fingerprints marred their chrome lids. No smudges stained the gray carpet at our feet.

Mama sat in front beside Cousin Grace. All we could see was the back of their heads. I watched the streets of town slip by and the desolate stretch of countryside begin. The fields and small patches of woods looked forsaken, forlorn. The trees were bare.

"Christina and Jason are coming tomorrow." Cousin Grace spoke to Mama in a somber tone.

Mama was silent. I couldn't see her face, but I thought she was probably worried. The family was gathering. *Shall we take a vote to send Aunt Sarah 'away'?* And Mama wouldn't want to.

"Is Paulie coming?" Trissy wriggled up and stood with her arms on the back of the front seat. Wisps of pale-brown hair poked out from the edges of her cap. She had lost a mitten on the train, but she didn't mind.

"Yes, Paulie's coming." Cousin Grace's voice gave no hint of her feelings. Last summer Paulie had broken a valuable vase. I think Cousin Grace was happier without big clumsy boys around.

But it wasn't her house, so it wasn't her place

to say "come" or "go." It was Aunt Sarah's house: every mahogany banister and latticed window and attic step, every long corridor and mantelpiece, and every door closing her in from the world outside. All Aunt Sarah's.

Whose house would it be if Aunt Sarah went "away"? I thought it would be nice if Cousin Grace could have the house. She deserved it. She had taken care of Aunt Sarah for many years.

But the house was too big for one graying, middle-aged lady. Aunt Christina and Uncle Jason thought the house should be sold and the money divided, along with Aunt Sarah's other money. I knew all about *that*. The grown-ups would have been surprised at how much I knew. Paulie had told me. "Someday we'll all be rich," he had bragged.

Cousin Grace turned off the road a mile or so farther on, and Aunt Sarah's house appeared through the trees. The winter winds that must have blown across the garden were gone now; thin gray rain fell through the twilight. It was a place I knew, yet did not know.

The sky was nearly dark, and lights shone at the windows.

I could see Aunt Sarah's windows, where a

dim light showed behind drawn curtains. She would be sitting there in her rocking chair. I wondered if she would come downstairs for dinner. I liked it better when she didn't come. But I wondered if she would.

Chapter 3

TRISSY AND I sat on the floor by the fire.

Full dark had fallen outside now, and the rain had stopped. Annie, the hired girl, was in the kitchen fixing dinner. It was a cozy moment in a gloomy house. I felt the room surrounding me like a cave of golden warmth in a countryside hushed now that the rain had stopped, lying blind under a starless sky.

Trissy's stockings drooped, a shoe was unlaced; the green of her dress cast reflections on her face in the firelight. I sat beside her, half listening to the low murmur of voices across the room. Mama and Cousin Grace were talking—

the same things I had heard so many times before.

"I know it's been hard on you, Grace," Mama said.

"Things just seem to get worse." There was a hopelessness in Cousin Grace's voice. "There's no way I can please her. She hardly goes out. And lately she doesn't want me to go out."

I glanced at Cousin Grace over my shoulder. What would it be like to live with someone who didn't want you to go out? I went out all the time: to school, with its echoing corridors and the sound of locker doors closing, with its notices on the bulletin board. . . .

"Hey, Alice, have you got the arithmetic? Sally Foster leaned close to me, showing her braces. *"Have you got the arithmetic, Alice?"*

And I went to Sunday school, dressed too tightly in good shoes and gloves. *"Can I wear your cologne, Mama?"* . . . Sunday mornings were stacks of newspapers Daddy was reading, coffee cake from the Elm Street bakery, Trissy hopping from foot to foot while she had ribbons tied in her hair, Mama asking, *"Do you remember your Bible verse?"*

"Let's go!" Daddy was ready with the car. Rain or shine, we went to Sunday school.

And we went shopping. We went to the library . . . to the dentist . . . ice skating at the park. We went to birthday parties. . . . *"Have you got a bow, Mama?"* From somewhere, marvelously, at the last moment, bows appeared for birthday presents for the girl next door, the girl two rows over at school, my best friend Margie.

Snowflakes struck our faces when we went out, sometimes rain and biting wind.

"Wait for me, Alice!"

"Hold my hand, Trissy!"

But we went *out*. Doors closed behind us. Hugs and kisses waited when we returned.

We had never lived with someone who didn't want us to go out.

"I told her someone has to do the shopping," Cousin Grace was saying. "But she doesn't listen."

"I know. . . ." Mama let the words drift off.

Cousin Grace sighed. She gazed down at her closed hands. She looked so sad and tired. The disappointments of a life I could only vaguely imagine were etched forever upon her quiet face. There was nothing she could hide. As long as I could remember, through all the summers of my life, she had been the same: Cousin

Grace, the poor relation who lived with Aunt Sarah.

"When Christina heard you were coming, she wanted to come too." Cousin Grace didn't lift her eyes as she spoke. "Christina thought we should all be here together to talk."

"I suppose so." Mama's voice was barely audible.

"Where's Skippy?" Trissy hopped up suddenly and wandered around the room, looking behind chairs, between table legs.

"Here, Skippy. Here, doggie."

"Yes, where is Skippy?" Mama was glad to change the subject.

"Skippy isn't here anymore," Cousin Grace said.

She said it like that because it's hard to say to a little girl like Trissy, "Skippy is dead."

Cousin Grace had a stiff, holding-back look on her face, and I thought maybe it made her want to cry to have to tell us Skippy was dead. The little dog had been hers, something in the house that was especially hers, not Aunt Sarah's.

"Where's Skippy?" Trissy wanted to *know*.

"Darling." Mama drew Trissy to her chair, her arm encircling Trissy's waist. I saw the flash of Mama's wedding ring on her slender finger. Diamonds catching firelight.

"He fell from the attic window." Cousin Grace's voice faltered. "The . . . the windows were open . . . to air the attic last fall. Somehow he got up there and fell out."

"Oh, I'm so sorry," Mama said in a hushed tone. She drew Trissy closer.

"Did he died?" Trissy's eyes were wide with wonder.

"Skippy's gone to heaven," Mama said gently.

Skippy's gone to heaven, Trissy. He went to heaven right straight out the attic window. Aunt Sarah pushed him.

And then Aunt Sarah was suddenly there in the room with us. We hadn't heard her coming. She stood in the doorway, gaunt and old—older than anyone I knew. Her heavy-lidded old eyes stared straight into mine.

"Aunt Sarah." Mama rose and went to greet her, holding Trissy's hand.

Aunt Sarah accepted Mama's kiss with indifference, as though it had never been given.

Mama was motioning to me, and I scrambled up.

"Alice is here, Aunt Sarah. See how tall she's getting."

Aunt Sarah had been closeted in her room when we came. Cousin Grace had tapped on the door, but Aunt Sarah had said, "Go away."

"Margaret and the children are here," Cousin Grace had called through the door.

"Leave me alone," Aunt Sarah had said. Cousin Grace had looked embarrassed, but Mama had touched her arm, smiling gently. "It's all right, Grace," she said.

"I want to see the dolls," Trissy had said, but Mama had herded us back along the hall, away from the closed door.

We had unpacked our suitcases and come downstairs to sit by the fire. And now Aunt Sarah had come to join us.

She was wearing a dressing gown and a shawl and soft bedroom slippers. She didn't look like a rich old lady. But she was.

She sat down in her chair by the fire and adjusted her shawl. "It's cold in this house," she complained.

"It's the damp," Mama soothed her. "It's this rain."

"I suppose you're right," Aunt Sarah grumbled. "I'm tired of the rain."

The conversation wasn't much. Mama did most of the talking. "We had such a nice ride on the train. . . . Alex was so sorry he couldn't come, he's so busy at his office just now. . . ."

Aunt Sarah nodded absently as Mama talked. And finally even Mama ran out of things to say. The room fell silent. I could hear the clock ticking on the mantel.

"Trissy wanted to see your dolls," Mama tried again, and the first spark of interest lit Aunt Sarah's eyes.

"Little girls like dolls," she whispered, thrusting her old furrowed face down toward Trissy.

Cousin Grace sat silent in her chair.

"Well, yes, of course they do," Mama agreed. Her voice was bright. "Is there time before dinner?"

Aunt Sarah didn't hear that. Or perhaps she didn't care whether there was time or not. She pushed up from the chair. Her shawl slipped to the floor, and Mama picked it up and put it around her shoulders again.

"Go along, Trissy," she said as Aunt Sarah started toward the door.

But now that she could go with Aunt Sarah to see the dolls, Trissy hung back shyly.

"Go along," Mama said again. "Alice is going."

I was going, but I didn't want to. My steps lagged as I followed Aunt Sarah up the stairs. I didn't like her room much. It was always stifling hot in the summertime, and often dark at midday with the shades down and the curtains drawn to keep out the sun. Ranged about in this dim summer twilight, amid the heavy claw-footed furniture, were the dolls. There were about twenty. One by one over the years Aunt Sarah had made them up in the attic and brought them down. Some were only ten or twelve inches high; some were larger. But they were all hideous. Their bodies were stuffed with rags and sewn together with haphazard stitching. A long arm, a short arm. Some dolls' arms were longer than their legs.

Aunt Sarah had made their clothes too, sewing them with uneven stitches from odds and ends of old velvet ribbon, cast-off dresses, scraps of once-white satin now aged and faded to yellow.

But it was their faces I dreaded most. Bulging foreheads and sunken cheeks, glass buttons sewn on for eyes—often too close together or with one eye higher than the other.

The mouths were drawn with a crimson crayon. Leering, lopsided grins drawn with a wobbly old hand gave them an evil look, as though a dire thing were about to happen. Some had a few strands of yarn hair, some had no hair at all, and one wore a dusty yellow wig Aunt Sarah had found in the attic.

Trissy hesitated at the doorway. No lamp was lighted in Aunt Sarah's room. There was only the firelight, glowing like the fire of a secret shrine. The dolls sat on the chairs and sofa, which were drawn to face the fire. In a far corner a tea tray had been placed on a night stand; a shapeless sweater was thrown over the footboard of the bed. Shadows wavered on the glass doors of the bookcase as Aunt Sarah passed. The fringe on a lampshade trembled.

Motioning us to come in, she settled herself in the only chair that was not filled with dolls. It was *her* chair, a worn rocker, and it creaked as she leaned back. There was nowhere else to sit. Trissy and I stood awkwardly before the fire.

"See who's come," Aunt Sarah said to the silent ring of faces. Glass eyes stared blankly. Crayon mouths grinned.

"Say hello," Aunt Sarah told us.

"Hello." Trissy's voice was hopeful. But the crayon mouths were silent.

"Say hello to Nellie." Aunt Sarah frowned at us as if we had done something wrong. We looked about uncertainly, and she pointed her finger at a small, particularly ugly doll with lean drooping arms and a bald head made from a piece of blue cloth.

"Nellie says hello to you." Aunt Sarah looked at us with a sly smile. The rocker creaked.

"I want to hear them talk." Trissy looked into Aunt Sarah's ancient face.

But Aunt Sarah shook her head.

"They only talk to me."

Trissy looked disappointed. She began to move slowly along the length of the sofa, peering at the dolls, trying to hear something.

"No one can fool me," Aunt Sarah said. "My dolls are always watching. My dolls . . . *Don't touch!*" She leaned forward abruptly as Trissy fingered a limp scrap of lace sewn to a doll's sleeve.

"Just look," Aunt Sarah whispered. "Don't touch."

We stood a few moments longer, and Aunt Sarah began to rock in the creaky old chair. I tried to think of something to say.

"Does it take you long to make a doll?"

She studied me for a moment. "Not long."

I hesitated. Her eyes were so deep, so old. But at last I said, "What do they tell you?"

"They warn me."

The firelight leaped, but the rest of the room was in shadow.

"About what?" I asked.

But Aunt Sarah didn't answer. She had closed her eyes. I didn't know what the dolls would warn her about. I didn't know who or what she thought might threaten or harm her. . . . Well, maybe Aunt Catherine and Uncle James. They wanted to put her "away."

Her eyes remained closed. I wondered if she had fallen asleep, and I took Trissy's hand. At the door I said "good-bye" just in case Aunt Sarah wasn't asleep, but not loud enough to wake her if she was. I thought we were lucky to get away so soon.

"I want to hear the dolls talk." Trissy tugged at my hand.

But I said we had to go downstairs. Dinner was probably ready by now.

"But I want to hear." Trissy trailed along beside me down the stairs.

"They don't *really* talk," I tried to explain.

But Trissy didn't understand. She still believed in Santa Claus and the Easter Bunny and fairies. In her kindergarten world dolls could talk. Her teddy bear really fell asleep in her arms at night. And someday a birdie would fly out of the sky and light on her finger.

Mama was sitting in a circle of lamplight. The draperies had been drawn at the windows, and the clock was chiming six. Cousin Grace sat with folded hands and the resigned expression of someone who has been treated unfairly by life and can't fight back. I thought it could not be easy or pleasant for her to live with Aunt Sarah day after day, year after year, with no life of her own at all.

But Cousin Grace smiled when she saw us coming, and when Trissy went to stand by her chair she smoothed Trissy's wispy hair and patted her arm.

"Are you hungry?" she asked.

I think Cousin Grace enjoyed our visits, skimpy as they were. We brought a little variety into her life.

But in a week we would be gone. The door would close behind us and Cousin Grace would be alone again with Aunt Sarah.

Chapter
4

AUNT CHRISTINA and Uncle Jason came the next afternoon. They had been driving since early morning. The blue Chevy was covered with mud.

Paulie was in the back seat. He had the door open even before the car stopped.

He's as bad as ever, I thought as I watched him get out of the car and dart aside to scare the sparrows. Trissy and I had just put bread crumbs on the feeder under the oak tree. The birds rose in a dark cloud, a flurry of wings against the leaden sky.

Paulie flapped his arms.

"Shoo! Shoo!"

He galloped after the birds.

Trissy ran out toward the car without a coat, but I stood by the door frowning at Paulie. I wished he would grow up and stop being so dumb.

Uncle Jason caught Trissy up in his arms, and Aunt Christina picked her way across the gravel drive, blowing kisses to Mama, Cousin Grace, and me, the reception committee at the door.

Aunt Christina was a small woman with short, fluffy brown hair and hazel eyes. She always wore kid gloves, stroking her fingers elegantly when she put them on. She was Mama's sister, and they looked quite alike. But Aunt Christina was more frivolous; she always spangled herself with jewelry and appeared faintly surprised that she was the mother of a big boy like Paulie. "Nobody believes I'm really his mother," she always said. She didn't care much for problems—which Daddy said was too bad, as we all have them.

Uncle Jason was strong and hearty. He was a painter. I had been to his studio once. Mama took me there one hot summer day, and afterward we had ice cream in a shop across the street.

I hadn't liked Uncle Jason's paintings much,

and the studio was a mess. Canvases were stacked against the walls, brushes stood in glass jars on a table wounded with the brown furrows of cigarette burns, and paint tubes were scattered everywhere, crushed, squeezed, oozing. I couldn't imagine Aunt Christina going there, bejeweled and perfumy, stroking her kid gloves. She was more suited to greeting guests at a gallery showing. I could imagine her in that setting more easily, quivering with bracelets and drinking champagne.

Uncle Jason had talked to us a lot about the motion of color. Blues receded. Yellows advanced. Reds clutched your heart.

I never knew exactly what he was talking about.

"I'll paint your portrait someday, Alice my darling," he had promised me. He caught my chin and tilted my face. "Ah, those blue, blue eyes. My Renoir girl."

Mama looked pleased that he thought I was beautiful.

"Maybe someday," she told Uncle Jason.

So I suppose someday he is going to paint my portrait. But it scares me a little, because he is so rough and hearty and I always feel small and defenseless when he is around.

He came striding along now with Trissy in

his arms, and there was a flurry of hugs and kisses when Aunt Christina came up the steps. Her silky raincoat rustled. A blue chiffon scarf floated at her throat. Paulie ignored everybody, standing on the sodden lawn gazing after the birds.

"Come on, Paulie," Aunt Christina called over her shoulder. And at last he did come thundering up the steps, a stocky, mischievous boy who couldn't care less about a hug from Mama and Aunt Grace. When Uncle Jason set Trissy down in the front hall, Paulie pulled off her hair ribbon and made her chase him to get it back.

"Play nice, Paulie," Aunt Christina scolded absently.

Uncle Jason wanted to know if Daddy had come, but Mama said he couldn't get away from his office just now, and then we all went into the living room.

Aunt Sarah was sitting in a wing chair by the fire. She had been there all morning. She said it was Tuesday so she wouldn't go out. No one had asked her to. I wondered what else she would say that was interesting, but she didn't say anything more.

"Christina and Jason are coming to see you," Cousin Grace had told her.

But she hadn't answered.

When we all came in and Aunt Sarah saw Paulie, she told him he couldn't see her dolls.

"You want to see my dolls, don't you? But you can't." She shook a finger at him. "Boys are rough. I don't like boys."

Aunt Christina bent and kissed Aunt Sarah's cheek. "How are you, darling?" she asked lightly.

"Only the girls can see my dolls."

"Of course, darling," Aunt Christina agreed.

"My dolls talk to me. They say no dogs, no boys." Aunt Sarah frowned at Paulie to show him there was no use begging to see.

Paulie got around behind Aunt Sarah's chair and stuck out his tongue at her.

"Can your dolls walk, too?" Trissy twisted a strand of hair and studied Aunt Sarah.

"No." Aunt Sarah's expression was wary. "I don't want them to go away. I want them with me."

Trissy tilted her head, staring curiously.

"Could you make a doll that could walk?"

"That'll be the day I leave," Uncle Jason joked in an undertone.

"Jason!" Aunt Christina shushed him. But I don't think Aunt Sarah heard.

Aunt Sarah didn't stay downstairs long after

35

that, and when she had gone upstairs and Cousin Grace went to speak to Annie in the kitchen, the discussion began.

"I see she's worse than ever." Aunt Christina drew off her kid gloves and ran her fingers through her hair like a comb to fluff it out.

"How Grace can stay here . . ." Uncle Jason shook his head.

"Where elso can she go?" Aunt Christina reminded him.

Mama looked weary. "Why don't you children go outside and get some fresh air," she said.

But we didn't go far. We listened behind the door. We couldn't hear everything, and what we did hear was pretty much the same old stuff we'd heard before. Some other arrangements must be made. . . . The house was too big. . . . Why Aunt Sarah wanted to keep it up, Aunt Christina would never understand.

"It's her home," Mama said.

Uncle Jason mumbled something I couldn't hear exactly . . . "incompetent to handle all that money"—something like that.

"Senile you mean," Aunt Christina said.

"Oh, no, not senile," Mama protested.

"Look how she talks to those dreadful dolls."

Aunt Christina's voice skimmed over the words, over Aunt Sarah's life, as though it were nothing of importance.

"She's always done that," Mama defended. "She's just lonely."

"Grace is here. Why should she be lonely?"

"That's not the point," Uncle Jason interrupted.

Then there was something about an appointment with a doctor.

"If she'll go." That was Aunt Christina.

"Do people still follow her when she goes out?" That was Uncle Jason.

Aunt Christina laughed softly. "Heaven help us," she said. I could picture her shaking her head and tangling her fingers in her necklace.

"Who follows her?" Trissy pulled at my skirt.

"No one," I said.

Paulie snickered. "Little green men with horns."

"What little green men?" Trissy's eyes were wide.

"No little green men." I glared at Paulie. "No one, Trissy. No one follows her."

Dear little Trissy. You didn't understand at all.

Chapter 5

THE RAIN BEGAN again the next day. Trissy and I went to the attic to dress up in old clothes. Paulie came too, because there was nothing else to do. But he didn't think dressing up was any great idea.

"Who wants to do that?" He shoved his hands in corduroy pockets and frowned around at the dusty corners of the attic.

"Cousin Grace said we could."

Paulie stuck out his tongue at me.

"Is this where Aunt Sarah makes her dolls?" He wandered over to a discarded old table that had probably been hauled up to the attic years and years before we were even born. It was littered with odds and ends of material, and I told him to leave it alone.

He lifted the lid of a wicker sewing basket on the table and pawed around inside.

"Leave it *alone*," I told him again.

"Who says?"

Paulie took a pair of scissors out of the basket and snapped them at me. The glinting blades flashed in the glare of the bare attic light bulb.

I turned my back on him and pulled at the lid of a trunk. I didn't care whether he played with us or not. I wished he'd stayed at home.

"Go away then," I grumbled. "Trissy and I are going to dress up."

I tugged at the heavy lid, and Trissy tried to help. "Watch your fingers," I warned her.

But the trunk lid was too much for us. "Come on, Paulie. Don't just stand there. *Help*."

He clacked the scissors a few more times to show he wasn't taking orders from me, but at last he put the scissors back in the sewing basket and came to help with the trunk. Between the three of us we got the lid raised.

Old clothes had been packed away inside: out-of-style dresses, a fan with a ribbon streamer, a straw hat. Paulie stood back with his hands in his pockets again, but Trissy and I hauled out the stuff. Near the top was a moth-eaten wool shawl with a tasseled fringe.

"I'm going to be a gypsy!" I put the shawl over my shoulders and swirled to make the tassles sway.

"I'm a gypsy too." Trissy had found another shawl. It straggled to the floor, covering her like a shroud.

"Why don't they throw all this junk away?" Paulie still wasn't interested.

Out from the old trunk came the stored-away years: the long-ago times before Aunt Sarah had grown old, before Cousin Grace had grown sad. There were men's shirts, waistcoats, cravats, collar studs. Here were the years when there had been brothers, uncles, grandfathers, a time when the house had been filled with people I had never known, never could know, a time when pipes were smoked and men looked at pocket watches and tall black hats were set down on the hall table.

The trunk held more than just old clothes. Covers fell from books with loose yellow pages. There were a box of buttons and a box of seashells. Someone had collected seashells once upon a time. I wondered who. There was needlepoint work begun and abandoned. A faded stagebill from some long-ago program. A cracked mirror with a mother-of-pearl back. How beautiful it must have been once.

"Hey, look at this!" At the very bottom of the trunk Paulie had finally seen something that interested him. It was a black eye patch on a thin elastic band, and he pulled it over his head. His blond hair was askew. His face was lighted with joy at his discovery.

"I'm going to be a pirate."

Then he found a long black coat and a red muffler, which he tied around his waist for a sash. He shoved aside Aunt Sarah's clutter of scraps and sat at her table to make himself a cardboard dagger to hang at his waist.

The box of jewelry was our greatest find, and we haggled over the pieces, dividing up the beads and rings, fastening our shawls with tarnished brooches.

"I want this. And this." Paulie snatched the best pieces. He had pushed the eye patch over his ear, to see better. He had forgotten he didn't want to play dress-up.

We foraged through the house, adding to the costumes we were getting together in the attic. Everyone was gone but Annie in the kitchen.

Everyone had gone with Aunt Sarah. It was supposed to be a routine checkup with her doctor, but there was more to it than that. I wondered if Aunt Sarah would come back or if the doctor would shut her up in a room with barred doors and we would never see her again.

"You can borrow this." Annie dredged down into the bottom of her shabby black purse and gave the "gypsies" a cheap lipstick. It was flattened, almost gone. But we loved it.

Annie's hair was frizzy, her wrists were white and bony. Her brother drove her out from town every morning in a rust-eaten car. She was "grown up" to me, but I don't suppose she was really very old. Her eyes sparkled with excitement as she helped us with our costumes.

"You can make rouge," she told us. She scrubbed her blunt fingertip into the lipstick and dabbed red circles on my cheek.

Good things were cooking on the stove, and the kitchen was warm and steamy. Annie's apron pocket bulged with pot holders. *I'll never forget you, Annie. I wonder where you are now, now that everything has changed.*

"There you go!" She rubbed lipstick on Trissy's cheeks. She gave Paulie a scarf, and he tied it on his forehead like a pirate's bandanna.

We rushed off, back to the attic, shawls trailing. Two gypsies and a pirate. We wanted to be ready to surprise everybody when they came home.

"They ought to be here soon," Paulie said.

I looked out the attic window. The rain was a thin veil in the early twilight. The surrounding woods and fields had a desolate look that chilled my heart. It was all so different from the shimmering, sunlit days of summer I knew so well.

I could see the road to town. But no car was coming yet. The ground was far below. The damp earth, the garden misty with rain—it made me feel queer to look down at it.

And then I noticed there were no sills on the attic windows.

How had Skippy fallen out?

There were no sills to jump up upon, to stand on, to fall from.

Only the small, high-set windows, flush with the wall.

Skippy went to heaven. He went to heaven right straight out the attic window.

I turned and saw Trissy making a smear on her mouth with the lipstick Annie had given us. She looked gnomelike in the drooping shawl and a hat with a dusty velvet rose. No one would know her now as she clutched her shawl with tiny fingers and smiled at me through the dark slash of lipstick.

"I'm ready." Paulie flourished his cardboard dagger. "Let's go down and wait."

"I'm ready," Trissy echoed. I spread my fan and covered my face.

We turned off the attic light and went down the narrow stairs.

Below lay the empty house with the clocks ticking on the mantels in its silent rooms.

Chapter
6

WE PULLED ASIDE the living room draperies and watched the road from town, hopeful at every shine of approaching car lights.

The minutes lagged. No one came. No passing car turned into our driveway as the late-afternoon light faded.

"Why don't they come?" Paulie complained. He fidgeted and frowned. He wanted to show off, and there wasn't any audience.

Trissy pressed her nose against the windowpane.

"I want Mama to see me," she said wistfully. Annie was busy now with preparations for dinner, and by and by we gave up our watch at the window and restlessly drifted upstairs. We were tired and disappointed, and already getting too warm in our costumes.

Annie had lighted the fire in Aunt Sarah's room, and through the half-open door we could see the dolls sitting in the firelight.

Aunt Sarah's room was forbidden territory, but Paulie was too irritated to care. He pushed the door open and stalked in. I held Trissy back, and we stood in the doorway watching him.

"Scaredy-cats," Paulie taunted us. His face was smug. "Come on. What are you afraid of?"

"I'm not afraid." I edged in just enough to show Paulie I wasn't.

He was looking around at Aunt Sarah's things. Pins rattled in a lacquered tray; a bureau drawer slid open with a faint whine. He picked up a small carved owl and examined it without interest. The silence of conspiracy hung in the room, as though Paulie and I were playing a game: who would dare stay longest in this forbidden place?

The sky was darkening rapidly now. Wind blew gusts of raindrops against the windowpanes.

46

"Do you think she'll come back?"

"You mean today?" Paulie sat down boldly in Aunt Sarah's chair. He sprawled out his legs and pointed his dagger at Trissy. "Sure she'll come back today," he said. "They'll lock her up all right, but not today. Those things take time."

"How do you know they'll lock her up?"

"My dad told me."

Mama had not told such secrets to me. She had only kissed me good-bye when she left. "Mind Trissy," she had said.

"She's crazy as a bedbug." Paulie got up and wandered around. I knew he was tired of waiting, hungry for dinner. He pushed his dagger through the lampshade fringe, making the silky strands ripple and quiver. He picked up a glass bowl and set it down. Dried rose petals fluttered to the floor.

"You're making a mess," I warned him.

"They're late," he grumbled. "And it's all her fault. Crazy old lady. Making these stupid dolls."

He seized one from the sofa and held it close to his face, wriggling his nose.

"That's Nellie." Trissy had come up beside him, trailing her shawl.

"Nellie, Nellie, smelly Nellie," Paulie chant-
ed. He shook the doll in Trissy's face.

"Why don't you just leave things alone," I
told him.

"I hate these old dolls," he said. He tossed
Nellie back on the sofa and snatched up another
doll. "I hate you," he said to it. "You're
ugly."

"Paulie, put it down."

He turned and looked at me.

"Put it down, put it down," he mimicked.
And then he turned and tossed it into the fire.

"Paulie—stop!"

I lunged forward, but it was too late.

Trissy and I stood paralyzed as the flames
licked around the sagging skirts, sucked at the
hideous face, consumed the doll before our
eyes.

"Paulie!"

But there was nothing I could do. The doll
was flaming, its glass eyes glaring bright
through the fire. And where Paulie stood at the
center of the hearthrug it seemed that every
doll in the room was staring at him. Glass-but-
ton eyes all turned toward Paulie from the
shadows beyond the firelight.

They saw you, Paulie. They saw what you did.

And then we heard the downstairs door and voices in the lower hall.

We fled from the room without a word, with no other thought but to get away. In the hall-way Trissy tripped over her long skirt, and I dragged her to her feet. Her eyes were wide with fright.

"Don't you say a *word!*" I had a good grip on her arm, and I shook her. Her face was pale and startled. Tears sprang into her eyes. But I had to make her understand.

"Not one word."

Paulie was gone—I didn't know where. And I didn't care. I pulled Trissy along the hall into our room, and dabbed at her tears with my shawl.

We were safe now. If anyone came upstairs, we were safe. We weren't in Aunt Sarah's room. We were in our own room.

I was sorry I'd been so rough with Trissy. My own heart had been pounding so hard I couldn't think. But as I dried her tears, I spoke more gently.

"Paulie didn't mean it, Trissy. He was just

tired because we've been waiting so long to show everybody our costumes."

Trissy sniffled. Tears hung in her eyes.

"Paulie wanted his mama and daddy to see his pirate costume, like you wanted Mama to see you. Paulie was just tired waiting so long and nobody *came*."

Trissy rubbed at her tears.

"We mustn't tell." I was whispering now. No one could hear us. Everyone else was far away in the other rooms of the house. But I whispered just the same. "We mustn't tell, Trissy. Understand? We mustn't tell. Aunt Sarah would be so mad at Paulie—and at us, too. We aren't supposed to go in her room."

"The dolls will tell." Trissy's voice trembled. "They talk to her."

"No they don't, Trissy. They don't really talk to her. Now *listen* to me. Promise you won't tell."

She gazed at me silently.

"Promise, Trissy!"

I looked into the tear-streaked little face. What could I say to make her understand?

"Promise you won't tell what happened." How many times would I have to say it?

"I promise," she whispered at last from the

gash of red lipstick. Little gypsy with the dusty velvet rose.

Chapter 7

AUNT CHRISTINA was drawing off her gloves, fluffing her hair. The living room was filled with voices and the smell of coats damp with rain. Umbrellas were propped open by the hall stairs to dry.

Mama stood by the fire, her coat still on. She looked small and defenseless in the confusion of people and voices around her.

"Such weather!" Aunt Christina looked distressed. Her shoes were spattered with mud.

"I didn't want to go," Aunt Sarah said.

Paulie pranced in the background, flourishing his cardboard dagger.

"I didn't like that man," Aunt Sarah said. No one was listening.

"Why, Paulie! My goodness, look at you!" Aunt Christina clasped her hands together. "Look, Jason. Look at this fierce pirate."

"And who is this?" Aunt Christina made a great show of not recognizing Trissy. She fingered the attic shawl, and a piece of tattered fringe came off in her fingers.

"Darling, you've been crying." Mama bent down and put her hand under Trissy's chin, tilting the small face up.

"A gypsy princess." Uncle Jason bowed to me. His dark eyes were alight with pleasure. He was very handsome with the firelight soft around him. Sometimes I liked him very much.

"Isn't that my fan?" Aunt Sarah frowned at me.

"It's just an old fan from the trunk in the attic, Auntie." Cousin Grace patted the withered hand draped upon the chair arm. "The children have been playing there. They couldn't go outside with all this rain."

Aunt Sarah looked at me a moment longer, not quite convinced. Then her thoughts strayed away from me. "I'm not going to that man again," she warned everybody.

I couldn't look at her. I was afraid if I met her eye she would know something was wrong.

Paulie was perspiring in the heavy black

coat. But he wouldn't take it off. He strutted around like a king. His red muffler-sash came loose and fell in a heap on the floor. He thought I had pulled it off, and he pushed me back against the sofa arm.

"Play nice, Paulie," Aunt Christina said.

Annie was bringing in wine, small goblets on a shiny black tray. The wine was deep red, like rubies. But there was none for us; it was only for the grown-ups.

"Well, here's to better times," Uncle Jason said, lifting his glass. He looked especially at Cousin Grace. She smiled wryly. I don't think she thought "better times" existed. Or if they did, she had given up hope they would come her way. Her small pearl earrings were her token of dressing up to go to town.

Aunt Christina, on the other hand, was jingling with bracelets. They slid merrily along her arm as she lifted her glass for the toast.

"To better times," she said agreeably.

Aunt Sarah drank her wine without a glance at anyone.

I sat on a chair arm, fiddling with my fan, feeling miserable. Paulie wouldn't look at me.

Uncle Jason poured himself another glass from the bottle on the tray.

"Take off your coat and stay awhile," he said

to Mama. The wine was making him jovial.

Aunt Christina nestled back into her chair and said, "It's been a long day."

It had been a long day for everyone, and Trissy fell asleep in a corner by the fire before Uncle Jason had finished his third glass of wine. Mama had to awaken her.

"Come, little gypsy. Supper time."

No one said anything about what had happened in town at the doctor's office. But Aunt Sarah had come home. Maybe they were going to lock her up someday, but they hadn't done it yet. By and by she would go to her room. By and by she would know what we had done.

That night I dreamed about Aunt Sarah's dolls. We were in a forsaken garden, wet with rain . . . and their voices whispered around me. But I couldn't understand what they were saying. I wanted to know, needed to know. It was so important. But the voices were only a blur of sound. *"Tell me!"* I begged. But the dolls only grinned.

The rain soaked their faces, glistened on the glass eyes, streaked the red crayon mouths. Everything ran together until their features were gone.

"Tell me! Tell me!"

But instead, they all grew silent. Their voices faded away like a vanishing whisper that I strained after and lost.

My eyes flew open. And with that rain-swept garden around me still, I heard Trissy's voice.

"Alice . . . " There was a tremor in her whisper. "Will the dolls tell?"

The garden, the rain, the dolls faded. I was in a big old-fashioned bed in a room in Aunt Sarah's house. The night lamp burned on a table by the window. A chair cast a shadow on the wall. A clock ticked. Mama was still downstairs. I had no idea whether I had been sleeping five minutes or five hours.

"Will the dolls tell?" Trissy's face hovered inches from mine. Mama had scrubbed her, but her lips were still stained with faint traces of lipstick. Strands of hair drooped over her eyes.

Let's go back, Trissy. Let's go back to the way things used to be. We always came in summertime. Remember, Trissy? And there were no fires then. The hearths are bare in the summertime. Cousin Grace lines up a row of plants on the bricks, no doll could burn in the summertime.

"Go to sleep." I smoothed back the wisps of hair. "I told you, the dolls can't really talk."

56

"But maybe they can." Trissy snuggled closer to me. "Maybe they'll tell on Paulie."

"No, they won't," I insisted. "And we won't either. Nobody tells. Do you understand?"

"But the dolls don't like Paulie anymore. He was mean."

"Go to sleep." I put a finger gently on each eyelid, the way Daddy always did. "Go to sleep," I whispered. "The sleep fairy is coming. . . ."

But after she fell asleep I lay awake, staring at the lamplight reflected in the window. There were two lamps, one inside our room, one outside in the night. And if I went to the window there would be two of me, Alice-in-the-room, Alice-in-the-dark-outside. I would be there, two of me, one on each side of the windowpane.

"You're still awake?" Mama sat down in the chair by the lamp that was burning inside our room and also burning outside in the darkness. She lifted her arms to unfasten a string of golden beads. I was drowsy, but awake, and I heard the familiar metallic sound of the beads being laid on the table.

"I thought you'd be asleep long ago." Mama bent over our bed. Trissy slept, her mouth half opened, her lashes fragile on her cheeks.

"Is anything wrong?" Mama touched my forehead. Did I have a fever? Always, since I was as little as Trissy, I could remember the gesture. Mama's first thought: feel the forehead. Is it hot, flushed, feverish? Is her beloved child sick?

Oh, I love you, Mama. You are always there when I need you. You love me.

"I was just thinking about Paulie."

Mama sat down on the edge of the bed. She fumbled with the clasp of her wristwatch, loosened the band, and slipped it off. She sat winding it for morning, listening to me.

"What were you thinking about Paulie?"

I didn't answer at once.

"Alice?"

"Oh, just why he's so—well, so bossy and mean all the time."

Mama laughed softly. "Did he do something bad today? I thought you had fun in the attic."

"We did."

"Your costumes were wonderful."

Mama sat holding the watch. I knew she was tired and wanted to get on with the things she had to do before she could go to bed. She always brushed her hair. She would put on a soft, rustling gown, a long gown. Gold slippers would show at the hem when she walked. She would brush her hair and put cream on her face. She would put her watch on the table beside the golden beads. Then she would go to sleep.

"Paulie isn't really a bad boy," Mama said. "Maybe he doesn't always 'play nice.' " She smiled with amusement as she used Aunt Christina's favorite phrase. *Play nice, Paulie,* Aunt Christina always said. *Play nice with the girls. Trissy is only little. Play nice, Paulie.*

"No," I said, "he doesn't always play nice."

Mama smiled again. And then she grew serious. "Remember when you had the measles last year? Remember the funny letter Paulie sent you? He wanted to cheer you up."

I remembered the letter very well—mostly because I hadn't expected a letter like that from Paulie. There was a clumsy drawing of somebody with a spotted face. Two big tears dripped down from the eyes. *"Heres some ridles for you,"* he had written under the picture.

Why does Alice have meesels?
Because she doesn't have mumps.
What has four legs and only one foot?
A bed. Thats where Alice is.

What has gold inside?
An egg. Thats what Alice eats.

They were pretty awful "ridles." But they made me laugh.

At the end of the letter he had written, *"Dont wory. I had meesels once. They went away ok."*

"I remember the letter," I said to Mama.

"Paulie has some lessons to learn, honey, about kindness and consideration. We all have lessons to learn. He'll grow up someday and be a good man."

She patted my cheek. "Go to sleep now."

She meant to comfort me, but I felt rebellious, trapped. I didn't want to hold things back from Mama. But I didn't want to be a tattletale either. And it was all Paulie's fault.

I hoped Mama was right. I hoped Paulie would grow up and be nice. But he wasn't grown up or nice *yet*. And it wasn't fair. I wanted him to be nice *now*. I wanted him to learn whatever lessons Mama thought he had to learn, and be nice *now*. I wanted to erase the whole evening. Play it over differently.

But the flames had curled around the doll's face. The skirts had caught fire and burned.

60

The melting crayon mouth had widened like a scream of pain.

The doll was gone. Destroyed. There was no going back, no changing things.

And Aunt Sarah was there now, in that room.

I dreaded morning. What a fuss there would be!

Chapter
8

To my surprise there was no "fuss." Morning came and went. Aunt Sarah did not come storming downstairs wailing that one of her dolls was gone.

I expected her at any moment, as I watched Paulie across the breakfast table. If he was worried, he didn't show it. I counted, and he ate nine pancakes while the grown-ups chattered . . . about how delicious the breakfast was, how awful the weather was. Uncle Jason said if winter came, could spring be far behind? Mama laughed and said apparently it was pretty far behind this year. Aunt Christina said she couldn't stay to wait for it, as they were leaving today.

My heart sank. I hadn't thought of that. Soon Paulie would be safely away. Only Trissy and I would be left to face Aunt Sarah and answer questions. *Yes, Aunt Sarah, we went in your room.* That confession would be hard enough. But what would I say when she wanted to know where her doll was. To say *Ask Paulie* wouldn't help much if he wasn't there to ask.

I had been dreading the moment Aunt Sarah would come downstairs. Now I wished she *would* come—before Paulie got away. But the minutes crept by, and Aunt Sarah did not appear. I knew she was awake. I had seen Annie pass the dining-room door, carrying up a breakfast tray with a teapot, a covered dish, and a napkin in a heavy silver ring. Annie's apron had a big bow in the back. Her hair was curled tighter than ever. Pretty Annie.

Uncle Jason poured cream in his coffee and lighted a cigarette.

"Make a smoke ring," Trissy begged. Her fingers were sticky with maple syrup and she licked them, smiling beguilingly at Uncle Jason.

"Don't lick your hands," Mama said.

Cousin Grace passed Trissy a napkin, but I didn't think that would help much. Trissy needed a good wet washcloth.

Uncle Jason blew smoke rings, and Trissy gave up licking her fingers and tried to poke them through the smoke rings.

"Smoking is a filthy habit," Aunt Christina said.

She was all in blue this morning, like a summer sky. Her jewelry was turquoise and silver. I thought it would be nice to be Aunt Christina. As calm and blue as a summer sky. I was waiting for Aunt Sarah, and I had six thumbs and a jumpy stomach.

Paulie took another pancake, and when he saw me watching he stuck out his tongue.

When breakfast was over and I could get him alone at last, I faced him accusingly. "Aren't you even sorry about what you did?"

"She'll never miss it." Paulie pushed at me. "She's got a whole roomful of those old dolls. How's she going to miss just one?"

We were standing by the stairway. Polished mahogany banisters curved up and away from us. Through the living-room doorway I could see Mama and Aunt Christina talking together by the window in low voices. No one could hear. They were talking about Aunt Sarah, I thought, and about going to the doctor yesterday. Mama was fiddling with her necklace the way she did when she was worried or nervous about something. Finally she walked away with a helpless gesture, as though she didn't want to talk anymore.

"Paulie—" Aunt Christina turned and saw us. "Have you got your things together? We'll be leaving soon."

Uncle Jason came down the stairs and set a suitcase in the hall where the umbrellas had dried the day before.

"Come on, pal." He ruffled Paulie's hair. "Get your things. Shake a leg."

It wasn't fair, I thought. Aunt Sarah would come down after Paulie left. I would be alone to face her.

Come down now, Aunt Sarah, I prayed.

But Aunt Sarah did not come down.

When Aunt Christina and Uncle Jason were ready to leave, they went upstairs to say good-bye to her.

"Come along, Paulie," Aunt Christina said,

putting her arm across his shoulders. I sat on the bottom step of the stairs, listening for an explosion when they got to Aunt Sarah's room.

No explosion came . . . only the silky rustle of Aunt Christina's raincoat as they all came downstairs a few minutes later. And I heard Aunt Christina's hushed whisper to Mama: "I don't think she really knows we're leaving."

"I don't think she even knows we've been here," Uncle Jason joked.

"Jason!" Aunt Christina chided him. She stroked on her kid gloves.

Paulie smirked at me with an I-told-you-so expression.

They had been to Aunt Sarah's room and nothing had happened.

Uncle Jason carried the bags out to the car, and Aunt Christina kissed Cousin Grace good-bye and told her not to worry. A pale sun came out, streaking the hall carpet. Mama gave Paulie a hug, but he didn't like that much and pulled away, jamming a cap down over his ears.

Annie stood by the dining-room door, smoothing her hands on her apron.

"You're as good a cook as ever." Aunt Christina blew her a kiss. But she didn't say, "See you next time," as she usually did.

66

Mama walked out on the porch with Aunt Christina, drawing her sweater about her shoulders and shivering in the chilly air. Paulie ran around the car with stiff outspread arms, pretending he was an airplane.

"Whhhrrrr, whhhrrrr." He tried to sound like an airplane, and Uncle Jason finally hauled him into the back seat of the car. Aunt Christina rolled her window down and called, "Good-bye, good-bye," one more time.

When the car had driven off, Trissy and I put on our coats and roamed the damp garden, sprinkling bread crumbs for the birds. Behind us the house loomed against the sky. The pale sunlight faded and disappeared.

"Here, birdie. Here, birdie," Trissy called up to the tree branches, straining her head back. The wind tossed her hair around her face and carried her thin little voice away.

On the other side of the garden birds began to fly down to get the bread crumbs we had left. Paulie couldn't scare them away today. But now that Paulie was actually gone, I began to miss him a little. I remembered his face flushed with excitement as he colored the cardboard black and cut out his dagger. I remembered how funny he looked with the eye patch shoved around over his ear.

As I stared up into the trees, I was startled to see a huge dark mass high overhead in the branches. It scared me for a moment, even though I realized almost at once what it was. I was seeing the squirrels' nest Cousin Grace had said was in the yard. I had never seen it before. You couldn't see it in the summer when the leaves were out, but I had known it was there. Sometimes we saw squirrels in the yard, and Cousin Grace had told me they had a nest in one of the trees. It gave me a queer feeling to look at it, revealed at last, far more gigantic than I had imagined it would be. There was something threatening about a nest so big. Surely some strange monster must live there. It was better to have it hidden by leaves, as sad things in life are hidden by daily routine. But I had seen it now, and I would always know how it looked fastened between the branches, dark and bulky and menacing.

"Here, birdie. Here, birdie," Trissy called.

At the far end of the garden, rocks formed the rim of what had once been a goldfish pool. As long as I could remember the pool had been dry, overgrown with weeds in the summertime. A few withered stalks still remained, and I sat on one of the rocks and tried to imagine what it had been like when goldfish were swimming in the water long ago.

Trissy came and stood on a rock beside me, shivering and looking for "birdies." But none came down to eat bread crumbs from her fingers. I wished it were summer now, so there would be flowers and we could watch the bees and play hide and seek in the grape arbor. By late afternoon the four o'clocks would come out. And the squirrels' nest would be hidden by leaves rustling in the sunlight.

"Can we be gypsies again?" Trissy trotted after me toward the house at last.

I didn't think it would be the same, just the two of us in the dusty attic.

"Maybe we can make fudge," I said. Annie had taught us one summer, and she always said our fudge was good—even when it was too soft and we had to eat it with a spoon.

"Goodness," Mama said as she met us at the door and saw Trissy's tangled hair. "You look like a waif. Alice, run upstairs and bring me the hairbrush."

The afternoon had grown gray, and the upstairs hall lay in shadow with a patch of flickering light. It came from Aunt Sarah's room, where the door stood slightly ajar. Aunt Sarah was in her chair, and I could see only the back of her head as she sat before the fire, the dolls ranged around her silent and watchful.

"No one can fool me, Aunt Sarah had said. *My dolls are always watching.*

The room was still except for the crackling of the fire.

I thought Aunt Sarah might sense me there in the doorway. I was afraid to breathe or take a step for fear she would turn and see me. But she sat straight, unmoving, as still as death. And then slowly her head moved forward, as though something had caught her attention, as though she were listening.

Firelight flickered on the grotesque faces, the crumpled skirts and stiff arms of the dolls.

And there was one dreadful empty place at the end of the sofa . . . where Paulie had picked up a doll.

Aunt Sarah's head bent toward the dolls, and my breath caught in my throat.

Were the dolls talking to her? Were they saying, *Paulie did it . . . Paulie did it . . . Paulie did it. . . ?*

There was something about the glimmering

room and the old lady with her head bent forward to listen that was worse than all the shouting and fussing I had expected.

"Alice, are you getting the hairbrush?" Mama's voice came from the foot of the stairs, floating up like a voice from a peaceful, normal world I had forgotten.

I turned and ran away down the hall.

Chapter 9

COUSIN GRACE drove us into town the next day, our first trip to town since we had come. Mama always wanted to go at least once. There was an antique shop she liked, and she would usually buy something. Then we would go to Lacey's Tearoom for lunch, and Trissy and I could choose whichever French pastry we wanted for dessert. It made up for waiting while Mama poked around among the brass candle snuffers and pewter jugs.

In the summer the door of the antique shop was propped open by a large cast-iron urn with tarnished metal rings set in the sides. Limp breaths of humid August air wafted in upon the old cane-bottomed chairs and coffee mills and lamps with colored glass shades. But now in this drear season of belated spring the door was closed against the cold. No one was sitting on the bench by the sidewalk.

Nothing was the same as in summer. There were no awnings rolled out over shop windows to keep off the sun. There were no store-front fruit bins, no children scampering along with ice cream cones dripping on flimsy summer shirts. The town, the street, the antique shop had a cheerless quality that depressed me. I wished I were home. I wanted to see Daddy and feed my turtles and go to sleep in my own bed. Most of all I didn't want to go back to Aunt Sarah's house.

Trissy and I followed Mama through the three rooms of the antique shop, fingering what didn't look too breakable.

Cousin Grace in her beaver coat stood talking to the woman who owned the shop. The woman listened intently to whatever Cousin Grace was saying, and nodded her head a lot.

On one table I found a large photograph album with a brown velvet cover. The pages were empty, and I wondered who had owned it and never once pasted in a picture. The velvet cover remined me of the album at Aunt Sarah's. The album was on a table by the living-room windows. It was covered with dark-blue velvet, worn at the edges. I had looked at it a lot. Every page was filled. Ladies and gentlemen of another time stood in gardens, on porches, beside old-fashioned cars. I had thought how hot it must have been for the women of those days, bundled up even in hottest summer with long skirts and high-necked dresses.

There was a picture of Aunt Sarah when she was about my age. I noticed it especially because it was the only picture of Aunt Sarah in the whole book. But to my disappointment it told me very little.

The picture had been taken in bad light. Aunt Sarah stood with her sister, now long dead and gone. The sister was smiling, but Aunt Sarah was just staring at the camera with a blank face. It made me wonder what she had been thinking about as she gazed like a stone image out of the murky photograph.

The picture had been taken on the front porch of the house where Aunt Sarah lived now, where she had always lived, where she probably had even been born a long time ago, when mothers had their babies at home. I wondered what she had been thinking when the picture was taken. Her face seemed to say, *I won't tell you.*

"Listen to this." Mama's hand, holding a music box, came between me and the empty pages of the brown velvet album. Tinkling strains of music began as she lifted the music-box lid.

"It's the 'Blue Danube' waltz," she said. Her face was full of delight, and she moved her head dreamily in time to the music.

Cousin Grace had come up beside us, and Mama said, "I've found what I want. Isn't it lovely?"

"Can we eat now?" Trissy looked up into the faces so far above her.

Cousin Grace bent down in her beaver coat and straightened Trissy's cap.

Mama closed the lid of the box, and the music stopped.

In the tearoom Mama took off her gloves and laid them beside her purse on the edge of the white linen cloth. Her blue-gray dress was just the color of her eyes. Earrings swayed when she turned her head.

Cousin Grace let her coat hang around her

shoulders. She lifted her water glass. Ice clinked softly as she set the glass back on the table, and she looked around with the pleased expression of someone who did not often sit so easily in midafternoon in places blazing with lights, humming with muted voices. On the walls were still lifes and landscape scenes in ornate gilded frames.

"You can probably sell some of the things at the antique shop," Mama said. She leaned forward, resting her elbows on the table, her graceful fingertips touching in a steeple.

Cousin Grace moved a spoon a few inches sideways and then back again. "I suppose so," she agreed without enthusiasm. "I don't like to think about all the details."

I pretended to be reading the menu, but I was listening. I knew they were talking about the day when Aunt Sarah would be "sent away." Then there would be that luxurious old house and its possessions to dispose of. I thought the lady at the antique shop would love it all. Someday other people, strangers, would sit by the fireplaces, climb the winding steps to the attic, put birdseed on the garden feeder—and maybe water back into the rock pound. But I would never see it.

Trissy wriggled in her chair, and Mama said, "Sit up straight, honey. Stop wiggling." . . . And I thought about Paulie throwing the doll in the fire.

I had been trying to think of everything else I could, but the burning doll kept coming back.

Paulie, stop! I had cried. But he hadn't stopped.

And even here in the red-carpeted tearoom I couldn't forget what had happened.

Cousin Grace excused herself to go to the ladies' room, and I whispered to Mama, "Is Aunt Sarah going away?"

Mama looked at me sadly from her beautiful blue-gray eyes. I wished she would look happy again, as she had looked listening to the music box, to the "Blue Danube" Waltz.

She shook her head and put a finger to her lips. I had touched a subject she didn't want to talk about.

"But what happened at the doctor's?"

"Nothing, darling. Look now." A dainty finger traced a line on the menu. "Have you decided what you want?"

Yes, Mama. I want to go home.

Trissy dropped a fork and ducked under the table to get it back. . . . Cousin Grace came walking along between the tables toward us. . . . I can see it all as clearly as though it were happening now. . . . I am sitting in the tearoom. And I can feel again that sense of changes coming and of grown-ups worrying about things I only dimly understood.

A waitress hovered above us with her pencil poised over an order pad.

"The crab salad, I think," Mama said politely, as if there were not another concern in her life but ordering lunch from the *Lacey's Tearoom* menu and then settling back in her chair to admire the landscapes on the wall.

Chapter 10

DADDY ALWAYS SAID there is no-body as easy to kid as yourself. Before we got home from town I had begun to think that may-be Paulie was right and Aunt Sarah hadn't missed just one doll. She hadn't said anything about it. She wasn't looking through the house for it. Everything would be okay. There was only one more day to go. Nothing had happened yet, and nothing would.

The things we had played with from the attic were still lying in a heap on the bedroom window seat, where Trissy and I had left them. I stood by the long mirror with one of the shawls draped over my shoulders. I spread the fan open and put it up to my face, peering dramatically over the fluted rim. I wondered what being a gypsy would be like. It was fun to think of traveling around in a wagon drawn by a strong black horse, sitting by campfires at night listening to violins.

But what did gypsies do when it rained? When it was cold? Did it snow in the land where the gypsies lived? Did they really kidnap babies and steal chickens and pierce their ears?

And could I, Alice, live a gypsy life, so wild and unprotected?

Finally I folded up the shawls, the long skirts, the fan, and lugged them all up the stairs again.

I opened the attic door and a flood of light startled me.

Aunt Sarah turned from her table with the alarmed motion of someone caught unawares. Light from the bare bulb fell full on her wretched old face.

I stood in the doorway with my armful of dress-up clothes and gaped with dismay to find her there.

Only one more day to go, I had thought. *Then everything will be okay.*

She had been working on something at the discarded walnut table, and she spread her hands out to hide what it was. But there was too much to hide. More scraps than ever littered the table's worn surface. The sewing basket spilled threads and pins. In the midst of all this lay a small bundle of cloth. She seized up the bundle and held it close. Her voice was a harsh whisper.

"Don't tell Grace."

I could only stare in confusion, and a hand shot out and took hold of my arm with a strong and pinching grip.

"Don't tell her. She doesn't like my dolls."

Aunt Sarah looked at me across the table with such a piercing, dreadful gaze that I felt as if my heart had stopped beating.

"I won't tell."

My mouth was dry. The words were a croak. I wanted to turn and flee back down the stairs. But she still held my arm. She was watching me intently to see if I was going to wrench away and run to tell her secret.

I had a sense of thoughts being formed and weighted in her mind . . . and then gradually I felt her grip loosen and fall away.

"It's for Paulie," she said. Her expression was furtive as she held out the object for me to see.

She had made another doll. She must have been working all day. As crudely as the doll was made, some time had been spent on it. The pirate costume was Paulie's in miniature. Red sash, black eye patch, bandanna tied around the forehead. She held it close even now, so I wouldn't touch it. But I didn't want to touch it. There was something fierce and vengeful about the one-eyed face, the sinister crayon mouth. The cloth she had used for the face was stark white.

"It's a present."

Her face at that moment looked quite insane to me. Quite mad. *Oh, yes. To begin with, Aunt Sara was mad.*

"And wait! See this." She fumbled in the pile of scraps that littered the table, lifted out the single blade of a small, curved manicure scissors, and stuck it into the doll's sash, as Paulie had put his dagger at his waist.

But this was no cardboard weapon. Aunt Sarah's eyes glinted as she looked at me for a moment. Then she took the blade from the sash and drew the sharp point across the back of her hand. A thin line of blood oozed out, and she looked up at me with a brooding eye.

Even now the whole scene has the unreality of a dream in my mind. But it was no dream. Everything was real and rawly clear in the blazing attic light.

"Go away," she said to me abruptly.

Still struck with awe, I didn't move at first. I had never seen anyone deliberately cut herself before.

"Go away," she said again. And the tone of her voice made me move at once.

I dumped the gypsy clothes on the trunk lid. A shawl slithered from the pile and fell to the floor, but I let it lie.

I left Aunt Sarah sitting there in the garish light, her head crooked low over her work.

Chapter 11

I WAS UNEASY all through dinner. I felt guilty every time I looked at Cousin Grace. *Don't tell Grace.* The words rang in my ears.

It seemed wrong to know something Cousin Grace didn't know—and wrong to be afraid to tell her. She was a sweet, forlorn woman, and a secret kept from her was a burden on my heart.

I saw Annie passing the door with a tray for Aunt Sarah.

I could picture Aunt Sarah sitting in her rocker upstairs. I thought that when Annie saw her she would think Aunt Sarah had been sitting rocking and dozing all day. Nothing more.

"Here's your dinner, Miss Sarah," Annie

would say brightly, thinking to herself, *Poor old lady, up here alone all the time*. Maybe she would tidy the room a bit, light the lamps, slide the napkin from the ring, and lift the cover from the plate.

Or maybe she wouldn't be thinking about Aunt Sarah at all. Annie carried up so many meals, it must be a dull routine for her by now. Maybe she thought about other things entirely while she went through the motions. *At seven I'm off to the movies with my new boyfriend. I'll wear my green dress. I'll kiss him good-night if he wants.*

I watched Cousin Grace slice the roast and pass back our plates with precise, unhurried movements. The plates were gold-rimmed and very old. They probably were very valuable. The lady at the antique shop might have them someday. And the silver, too. It was heavy, patterned with curving flowers and an initial so elaborately drawn I could only assume it was a *W* for *Winfield*, Aunt Sarah's family. The silver gleamed on the white cloth. Annie kept it well polished.

Cousin Grace ate with the same unhurried gentility with which she had carved the roast and passed back the plates. Cranberry relish burned red in a cut-glass bowl. I saw Annie walk by the door again, going back to the kitchen.

Trissy and I lay on the floor in front of the fire that night, for one last time. By tomorrow night we would be boarding the train for home. And we might never see this house quite the same again, or ever lie by the fire.

Trissy fell asleep lying there, and Mama said, "She's had a busy day."

In the flames I began to see the doll burning again. And I gazed hypnotized by the tricks the fire played. She was there, burning in the red glow of the living-room fire. I could see the ring of mute, glass-eyed faces—the other dolls. Now they seemed real to me. Alive. Watching. Feeling the horror of what was happening.

Their companion was burning before their eyes.

But how helpless they were.

If they could have moved, walked, would they have thrown themselves at Paulie, clawing, scratching, kicking . . . pushing *him* toward the flames?

Can your dolls walk, too? Trissy had asked.

No . . . I want them with me, Aunt Sarah had said.

So the dolls could not move. They could only talk, and only to Aunt Sarah. From the ring of distorted faces that surrounded her, from smeary crayon mouths, had revenge come. . . . *Paulie did it. Paulie threw her in the fire. Punish Paulie—punish Paulie—punish Paulie.*

Could you make a doll that could walk? Trissy had asked.

But Aunt Sarah had not answered.

I closed my eyes to shut out the burning doll. The living room was very quiet. No outside sounds intruded. No bird call or car horn. The country was always so quiet at night . . . as I think graveyards must be.

"Mama, Aunt Sarah is making a doll for Paulie."

Trissy was sleeping. Cousin Grace had gone to the kitchen to speak with Annie. Mama and I were alone, and at last the scene in the attic was too much to bear by myself. I had to tell Mama. Aunt Sarah had only said, "Don't tell Grace."

"What did you say, Alice?" Mama looked up

with an absent expression.

"Aunt Sarah is making a doll for Paulie."

"She is?" Mama tried to bring her thoughts back from some faraway place. "I didn't know she ever gave away any of her dolls."

Listen, Mama. I'm trying to tell you something.

"It's a pirate—like Paulie was that night."

"Mmmm." Mama nodded her head and murmured, "That's nice," but I knew she had other things on her mind. She was realizing now that Aunt Sarah must go away. She was concerned about details, about the house, the furniture, where Cousin Grace would go. I don't think she thought anymore at all about the pirate doll, the doll for Paulie.

As far as I know, I am the only one who saw the doll, except Aunt Sarah herself. And I only saw it that one time, in the attic. The next morning it was already wrapped up in stiff brown paper, tied with twine, ready to be mailed. Paulie's name and address were printed on the brown paper with black crayon.

Aunt Sarah brought the package down to the kitchen. Cousin Grace stood buttoning her coat, ready for a few morning errands in town.

Breakfast was over, but the spicy smell of sausage still lingered in the kitchen, and Annie had opened a window to let in fresh air. The yellow curtains stirred lightly in the breeze. Mama and Trissy were in back by the grape arbor. Birds chattered in the bare trees above their heads, and the sky was gray like doves' wings.

"What's this?"

Cousin Grace took the brown package Aunt Sarah thrust toward her, and read the name.

"Paul Redding . . . ?"

"It's a present," Aunt Sarah said.

I tried to look everywhere in the kitchen but at Aunt Sarah. I looked at Annie, running water into a foamy dishpan . . . at the clock on the wall . . . at the plants on the windowsills . . . at the pantry door, which stood ajar, so that I could see the shelves of canned goods and the bushel basket of apples and the cups hung on hooks all in a row.

Mama and Trissy were coming back, hand in hand along the flagstones.

And when I looked at the kitchen again, Aunt Sarah was gone. Not far. I saw her sitting in the living room by the fire, looking into the flames.

Mama and Trissy came in, laughing about something. A gust of cool spring air rushed in as the door opened.

"Well," Cousin Grace shook her head with weary patience, "I'll have to go by the post office and send this off."

Mama was listening sympathetically.

"There are no parking places there," Cousin Grace said. I had a feeling she would like to dump the parcel into the nearest wastepaper basket. "At least it's hardly ever possible to find one."

Mama understood. All grown-ups understand parking problems.

"Alice can go along with you," Mama suggested. "She can run in and mail the package, and you won't have to worry about parking."

"Get your coat, honey," Mama said.

Cousin Grace looked at me hopefully.

And I went through the hall, past the dining room, where a forgotten coffee cup sat on the long white tablecloth, past the living-room door. I saw Aunt Sarah by the fire. Up the curving stairway I went—past rooms with closed doors and walls hung with portraits of people I'd never known and never would know.

90

Chapter
12

I GOT INTO THE CAR with Cousin Grace. It was my first time ever to sit in the front seat with her. Mama always sat there, and Trissy and I sat in the back.

The road to town was dulled and weather-beaten by winter snows and spring rains. We passed only a few cars and a few isolated houses. A vast silence surrounded us, spreading over the meadows and groves of trees. The package lay on the seat between us, beside Cousin Grace's purse.

Cousin Grace did not talk to me. She never did talk much. I peeked sometimes at her soft profile, and I watched her hands on the wheel.

No wedding ring with diamonds sparkled there, as on Mama's hand. Her nails were short and pale. I wondered if she ever wore polish. It didn't seem likely.

As I saw those hands, her whole life seemed to spread out before me with all its rejections and loneliness. Hours in the gloomy house, meals alone at the dining-room table, where the only sound was her own fork upon her own plate. Annie served her, but Annie's footsteps made no sound on the carpets. *Talk with me, laugh with me, sing with me . . . somebody!* But there was only the wind at the windows, the delicate ring of a cup set back upon a saucer.

Her life-to-come was closed off from view by a shadowy curtain of uncertainty through which I could not see.

The countryside sped by like a bleak painting that would have found no home in Uncle Jason's studio, where all the canvases were vivid with blues and yellows and reds that "clutched your heart."

Our scene was gray as far as the eye could see. A flock of birds wheeled over leafless trees.

We were just reaching town when Cousin Grace said, "I wonder what's in that package."

She didn't really look at me. Cousin Grace was one of those drivers who keep their eyes on the road ahead. She made a turn, slowing to a stop for a station wagon that was pulling into a parking space by a hardware store.

I pretended to be looking around at everything so I wouldn't have to answer.

The station wagon parked, and we moved on. And then, suddenly, a stray dog ran into the street ahead of us. Cousin Grace slammed on the brakes, and Aunt Sarah's package slid to the floor.

The dog ran on safely, but our car stayed still. I looked at Cousin Grace to see why she was waiting. She was looking after the dog. Tears glistened in her eyes, and she reached for her purse.

"I'm sorry, Alice. You mustn't mind me." She found a handkerchief. "I just miss Skippy. . . ."

She wiped at the tears. A car honked behind us, and we moved forward at last.

"I'm sorry Skippy died," I said awkwardly. Seeing grown-ups cry always made me feel embarrassed.

Cousin Grace didn't take her eyes off the traffic. I wanted to ask her about the attic windows that had no sills. I wanted to ask her what had really happened. But I didn't know how to start. She pulled to a stop in front of the post office, and took advantage of the pause to brush at her tears again. It was time to mail Aunt Sarah's package.

"Now where is it—? Oh, here it is." Cousin Grace leaned down and rescued the package from the floor of the car. She held it in her hands for a moment. The paper crinkled as she touched it.

"Does Aunt Sarah miss Skippy?"

Cousin Grace looked away.

"No, I'm sure she doesn't." There was bitterness in her voice. "Aunt Sarah didn't like Skippy. He chewed up one of her dolls."

I took the package. But I sat holding it in my lap, thinking about Skippy. *Skippy went to heaven right straight out the attic window.*

"Here, this should be enough." Cousin Grace put two one-dollar bills into my hand. "Run in now, and I'll drive around the block. I can't park. Look for me when you come out."

The post office was small, and the air reeked of pipe tobacco.

The man standing ahead of me in line was the culprit, and the woman in front of him kept looking back over her shoulder with sniffs of disapproval.

Only one mailing window was open, and it's hard to explain the feeling I had as I waited in line. The hand on a clock on the wall jerked forward each time a minute was up. Someone came out of a room beyond, letting the door open briefly and then close on a vista of mail carts and cluttered shelves.

But I noticed all of this only automatially. A rush of apprehension swept over me. Casting reason aside, I let all the fears and worries I had been trying to deny rush in.

Can your dolls walk, too? Trissy had asked.

No . . . I want them with me, Aunt Sarah had said.

But what if Aunt Sarah had really made a doll that could move? A pirate doll, to remind Paulie of that night. A pirate doll with a sharp dagger stuck into the red waist sash.

Paulie did it. Paulie threw her in the fire. Punish Paulie—punish Paulie—punish Paulie.

Suddenly I felt quite small and frightened. The people in the post office towered around me. I was so small, only a little girl compared to them. The package throbbed in my hands, and I found myself gripping it tighter to hold it steady. I thought at any moment it would lunge from my hands with a life of its own.

Don't mail this to Paulie, a voice inside me cried. *Don't mail this to Paulie.*

"Your turn, girlie."

The man behind the counter stared down at me.

I couldn't answer.

"What'll it be?" There was a tinge of impatience in his voice.

I looked up at him, and then I jammed the package inside my coat and ran out to meet Cousin Grace.

The bundle felt as big as a barn, and Cousin Grace looked at me curiously as I got into the car.

"You're so pale, Alice. Is anything wrong?"

"There was a man smoking a pipe," I mumbled. "It made me feel funny."

"I shouldn't wonder," Cousin Grace agreed. "Nasty things."

And we started home.

Panic swept through me. What had I done? I had been sent to mail a package, and I hadn't done it. What had come over me? There was no such thing as a doll that could move. . . . But how could I tell anyone what I had done? Who would understand the fearful feeling that had engulfed me? How could I explain? There was no way. I sat huddled on the seat beside Cousin Grace, crouching over my bulky coat.

It was an ugly present. Paulie wouldn't want it, I reasoned frantically.

But that still didn't excuse my disobedience.

What was I going to do now?

My mind raced.

Whom could I tell?

Nobody.

And I still had Cousin Grace's two dollars.

Chapter 13

OUR VISIT to Aunt Sarah's came to an end. We left as we had come, under chill, dark skies. There was no real sign of spring coming yet.

Cousin Grace drove us to the station late in the afternoon. I sat in the back seat of the car with Trissy. Mama and Cousin Grace sat in front. All we could see was the back of their heads. They hardly talked at all. Even Trissy was subdued, silent. I tried to think about seeing Daddy again and calling my girl friends. And what fun it would be being on a train overnight! Mama didn't like to fly. Otherwise, we would be home sooner.

At the station Mama hugged Cousin Grace.

"I'll be in touch," she said. "Try not to worry."

Cousin Grace kissed me good-bye. I felt the softness of her coat and smelled the sweet scent of lilac cologne.

"Come and see me soon, Alice," she said kindly.

But we did not return until late summer. And by then everything had changed. All my premonitions had been right: we never saw the house again as it had been for so many summer visits in my memory. We never saw it again at all except for that one last time in late summer.

Aunt Sarah had been gone since May. Even Mama had at last agreed it was probably the best thing to do (*the only* thing to do, Daddy said). Paulie told me they had let Aunt Sarah take her dolls with her. "That's all she cares about, anyway," Paulie said. He had heard his mother say that, I suppose.

Cousin Grace had been staying on at the house to take care of arrangements, and when the house was sold, Mama said she would come to help with all the many details—sorting stuff, selling furniture, the hundred and one things that had to be done.

I went to the garden that first afternoon of

our last visit. It was a hot, airless day. There was not a cloud in all the high expanse of radiant sky that spread above the parched fields and drooping flowers. Unrelenting heat bore down. The whole landscape shimmered with light and heat and blue reflections from the sky.

I went to the garden out of curiosity. Had anyone discovered what I had done? Had anyone found the brown paper package I had buried by the rock pond?

I had come back from my trip to town with Cousin Grace that cold spring morning, confused and dismayed. Mama was packing. Trissy sat on the edge of the bed, winding up the music box. Strains of the "Blue Danube" waltz drifted through the bedroom.

The suitcases were open on the bed, partly packed already. Our visit was at an end. Next week I would be back in school, adding up arithmetic problems, separating verbs from nouns.

"Hold this, darling." Mama had given a sweater to Trissy. She would find room for it in a suitcase later. I stood watching, with the package hidden under my coat.

Cousin Grace's two dollars for postage loomed, as large a problem as the brown parcel.

Winding down, the notes of the "Blue Danube" waltz grew slower and slower . . . and finally stopped.

"Put it here."

Mama moved aside some things in her suitcase, and Trissy tucked in the music box. The "Blue Danube" waltz was silent.

I ran out to the garden and scratched a hole in the ground by the pool. The dirt was hard and cold. It packed under my fingernails. I shoved the doll I hadn't mailed into the shallow hole and patted dirt back over the top.

Later I gave the two dollars to a Salvation Army kettle.

"Thank you, miss," said the bare, plain woman standing beside it. She had a blue cape and a clanging bell, and her hazel eyes were like Aunt Christina's.

I tried to think that Cousin Grace wouldn't mind her two dollars being given away for a good cause.

And I tried to think that what I had done wouldn't ever matter.

But now we were back at Aunt Sarah's.

I stood by the rocks where I had dug the hole. Summer weeds had grown up again where there had been only frozen winter ground.

Leaves had already begun to fall as August ended. They covered the ground. But not so many leaves had fallen that I could see the squirrels' nest in the branches of the tree at the end of the garden. It was still hidden. I could only see it in my mind. It scared me still.

I knelt and pushed at the leaves that had fallen, and when I had scattered them aside I saw a ragged hole in the ground where there should have been my mound of patted-down earth. Lying in the hole were the remains of the brown wrapping paper of the package I had buried.

The paper was slashed and cut as though by a sharp instrument wielded with frantic strokes. It was torn and hacked, with a gaping hole in the center cut out by desperate blows.

Nothing remained but the shreds of paper.

There was no pirate doll inside.

I felt a quiver along my arms, and I looked about with dread, expecting something to rush at me from the parched summer grass, something that shrieked, and flourished a curved blade.

But whatever had escaped from the package I had buried was long gone from the garden.

There was not a sound or movement in the

grass except the hot August wind. A bird called overhead. Nothing more.

I turned and looked at the house. What would become of it now?

What would become of Cousin Grace?

I would never be back. I knew that. I would never see Aunt Sarah's house again. I looked at it a long time to fix it in my mind—at the way it rose against the sky, at its gables and windows and chimneys. Sunlight rested on it harshly, glaring at windows that shielded gloomy rooms. And I saw the windows of Aunt Sarah's room, with the curtains drawn as they always were in summer. But she was not in that room now. She was gone. And the dolls were gone.

Aunt Sarah lived in a world I could never know, a world different from mine, a world where things happened that I could not understand.

I saved your life, Paulie. Grow up and be a nice person.

"Alice."

Mama called me, and I ran across the garden.